UNDER THE MOONLIGHT

Harrison Okhueleigbe

For Nẹnẹ́, whose strength and endurance over the years have inspired me; her memory, forever in our hearts.

Contents

Preface vi

Part One 1

Chapter One 2
   Dreams and Imaginations 2

Chapter Two 12
   Family 12

Chapter Three 30
   Anticipation 30

Chapter Four 42
   The Arrival 42

Chapter Five 62
   Awakening 62

Part Two 67

Chapter Six 68
   A Land Far, Far Away 68

Chapter Seven 76
   The Unknown 76

Chapter Eight. 84

    Prisoner. 84

Chapter Nine 88

    The Reveal 88

Chapter Ten 94

    "One of Us" 94

Chapter Eleven. 100

    Strange Voice 100

Chapter Twelve 108

    Reunion 108

Part Three. 113

Chapter Thirteen. 114

    Midnight Moon 114

About The Author 124

Endnotes 125

Preface

I really do think autobiographies are long boring historical accounts. While I will never write a history of my life, many things and events have had such a tremendous impression on me and have shaped my very being, personality and reality today.

A memoir then? Yes, I can do that!

"Under the Moonlight" is a two-part story of the artist as a child living with his family in suburban Lagos during the '90s, as he anticipates and experiences his grandmother's visit.

The first part introduces the reader to the child and his family, the dynamic there, and the world he created and coloured in his imagination.

The second part portrays the exciting fictional world where humans and spirits either coexisted or communicated in some way, exploring themes like envy and perseverance.

With the plot moving between events in my childhood and the world of the folktale characters, I have embellished it with my own thoughts and how I imagine things must have been growing up.

I've kept the tone informal, with many parts of it in Nigerian English, so as to express the language and culture of the setting. As a result, I have provided end notes to many not-so-familiar words and phrases, accompanying songs, poems and proverbs.

I don't know if you would find these accounts funny, interesting, painful or ridiculous. I suppose, though, that you may also find yourself remembering with nostalgia what childhood was, and definitely means for you today as you read along!

Part One

Chapter *One*

DREAMS AND IMAGINATIONS

My mum was standing by the door at the entrance of the house, hands akimbo, yelling for me to come inside.

"You're still outside, boy? Don't make me come call you a third time. It's already midnight and you're still out here! The mosquitoes will have had their fill feasting on you, then you end up in the hospital with malaria. No, you won't put me through that ordeal again. Now get up and get in!"

My recent exploits of jumping off an eleven-foot wall whilst pretending to be Spiderman[1] had left me with a dislocated wrist and had also left my mother impatient and anxious, but I didn't want to come in. I wanted to stay outside and daydream under the night sky.

I had spent the last four hours lying outside in the yard. For the first three hours, my family had been with me, receiving fresh air as most families in Nigeria do, especially during the six month-long West African dry season. At this time of year, the brick buildings had stored up so much heat that staying indoors in the early hours of the evening felt like being in a masonry oven. With limited ventilation and electric fans and air conditioners regularly out of action due to power shortages, it was routine to allow time for the walls to cool off before families retired inside for the night. These nights were usually good bonding moments. Many households would have their evening meals together in the open. With the night brightened by the full blue moon, children played night games such as Ayò Ọlọ́pọ́n,[2] and older family members told riveting tales, all while enjoying the cool steady breeze of the evening. I longed for these moments.

I loved being outside the house at night-time. Our compound was a large space of private property in rural Lagos, before it became a bustling metropolis. My father said he purchased it from the government at a giveaway price before he had any of his children. He had built a simple structure that brought all the comforts of home and held unforgettable memories.

We were a family of seven. I had two older brothers and two younger sisters. I like to think we lived on a farm, as we had a garden to the east of the yard where we planted corn, groundnuts, plantain,[3] and all the vegetables we needed for our meals. My favourite among these was the Efirin,[4] a species of scented leaves that filled the surrounding atmosphere with their aroma at night. To the north of the garden was a small poultry farm where we reared chickens; I still remember how they all descended from the first *patriarch and matriarch of our chicken dynasty.*[5] To the west of the compound were different trees: mango, guava, the Egyptian Balsam, almond, and coconut. The last two were a symbol of pride for me; I had planted, nurtured, and watched them become fruit-producing giants. Much of the ground was covered in a carpet grass that provided green flooring for the compound. It was a nice area for football, although our parents forbade my siblings and me from playing. They were wary of the glass louvres. Kids our age could be very clumsy. A few years ago, in fact, we had damaged those of the living room. We still had a hidden ball, which we played with, however, when there were no adults around, albeit with much care.

Tonight, at about the last hour before midnight, as was customary, my siblings had rolled up the mats on which everyone had sat, but I had stayed back. This was my me time, the time when my imagination came alive and when the compound became my sanctuary. At this time, I became the *alpha and the omega[6]*—everything came alive, all the elements in the natural world became animated, and somehow I felt that we could communicate with them. I even had names for most of the things around me. In my mind, we were all neighbours—me, the moon and stars above, the night birds, the vegetation and trees around, even the wind. There was a steady and harmonic rhythm in the air as leaves and branches swayed back and forth in the gentle night breeze. In my small world of fantasy, we all lived happily, complementing one another. Life was beautiful in my little paradise.

My mind would wander on these nights as I lay face up, staring at the moon, with its different shapes and sizes—full, half, and crescent—wondering what sort of neighbour it was.

"Do you ever quarrel with the sun? Do you wish it was never this hot? I hope you both live in peace," I would whisper.

Before I began imagining it as being alive, I used to call the moon the silver calabash hanging in the clouds. It was not as close as the trees and wind, so I tried to imagine how other heavenly bodies interacted with it. I did learn from school that it was illuminated by the sun, thus giving us a bit of light in the cool of the night. The entire collection of constellations before me were alive, and I would think the twinkling stars became more and more familiar with each passing night. Every time I gazed at them, wide-eyed, almost never blinking, I spotted their familiar features. I could swear I recognized most of them from previous nights.

Tonight, however, I had not only been entranced by the present moment, but I was also thinking about what fun and adventure would be held yet for me in the coming days. I had heard my mother and father earlier in the week talk of a visitation by my grandma, and a letter had come from my hometown village where she lived, confirming her visit for the following week. My siblings and I could not wait, as we counted down the days leading to the D-day. My eagerness, as usual, was matched with fantasies and imagination.

Mum had hinted what to expect from grandma; it was not the first time she had visited, although I was still a toddler during her last visit and had no memories of it. Curiosity had led me to ask my mother plenty of questions, and even though she could not keep up with me, she was graceful and patient enough to tell me about the night-time stories. She told me of her childhood, growing up in the village, how her mother, my grandma, would gather kids in the neighbourhood, sit them under a star apple tree, and tell mythical stories.

"These were the best parts of my childhood, and I never forget those moments," said my mother.

"The darkness of the night, the whaling of the tree leaves, the clicks of bats as they circled around the tree as if to eavesdrop on the conversations, the owls sitting pretty on the rooftop, gazing at us, wide-eyed and hooting away, inadvertently adding melody to the folk songs that followed the tales," she continued, this time with visible nostalgia.

As I lay on my mat, all I could do was dream while she spoke, placing myself in the setting, albeit in my own compound here in Lagos. The days could not go by quicker.

Slowly, but reluctantly, I slid off the mat on which I lay, rolled it up, strung it with twine, and held it to my chest with my left arm as I gently walked past my mum who had stood there all the while, now holding open the door with her left hand, leaving the right on her waist. This time she made sure I went in, and she locked the door behind me with a padlock, the key of which only she knew where it was ever kept. I dragged my weary body up to bed.

Only one day to go.

Chapter *Two*

FAMILY

"The Voice of America, VOA!"[7]

I grabbed the pillow to block my ears against the sound from my dad's transistor radio. I should have gotten used to it, as this was a daily routine for my dad while he got ready for work. The VOA jingle was a familiar one, it had become like a daily alarm. There was no escaping the radio at this time, no matter where you were in the house. But it was not the voice of the reporter over the radio that was the most annoying, it was the hissing sound the vintage device constantly made while he tried to tune it to his desired frequency and station that made sleeping at such a crucial time in the morning impossible. My father had the routine of listening to the VOA first thing in the morning and the British Broadcasting Corporation later. At about when he was stepping out of the house and having his parting words with my mum, who would always be awake to get his breakfast ready, Don Williams[8] was playing on the radio. By this time, I was already fully awake and enjoying the songs. Don Williams was my favourite country music artist.

"...you're my anchor in life's ocean. But most of all, you're my best friend,"[9] I muttered the final words of the best part of my favourite among his songs.

Today I carefully eavesdropped on the conversation between my parents. My mum reminded him of the need to get some extra provisions for her mother's arrival. His final words to her were not the expected cordial farewell you would see on a soap opera, it sounded more like him giving instructions.

"This room will have to be cleaned out and rearranged before her arrival," he said, staring in the direction of the bed where I lay. Then he left for work.

He was a candid man, brusque in manner and hardly was in touch with his emotional side. I always wondered how they met and got married anyway. I remember my mum telling me about it one time, but I became disinterested, it sounded nothing like a Cinderella story. She told me before they met he was so ambitious that he sought to travel abroad for higher education and a better life.

"He could have been living in England," my mum would say reminiscently.

"But he's made something of himself here and things aren't so bad."

Besides, he probably wouldn't have met and married you and had us kids had he left, I thought to myself.

My father was not your conventional daddy type. The only time I remember him laughing, and, perhaps, the only time we ever shared a spirited moment was when we both danced at his office's Christmas party when I was six. We probably never got along so well as I grew older. Although I hated our relationship, I loved the man himself. Though he never expressed his love and pride for me verbally, somehow I knew he had it in him. Even as a preteen, I could sense he was a responsible man, never abdicating his God-given duty to his family. He was not the biggest man physically, yet he was the strongest man you would ever meet. He was strong mentally and emotionally. Once, when we fell on hard times and our family seemed like a boat in the vast sea being tossed here and there by a storm, and you would think it was going to sink, my father, the helmsman, the finest there is, somehow steered the sail to gentle waters. With limited resources, he put us through the best schools in the neighbourhood. Education was so important to him; it was the key to unlocking the future.

"Aren't you going to get up and start the day? It's past seven already," Mum said to me, dragging the sheet off my body.

"Ooooh, but we're on holiday, why do we have to wake up so early?" I protested.

"Because you've got chores. You and your siblings will have to assist in getting things ready for Grandma," she said with a smile on her face, as if knowing that would get me off the bed to do her bidding.

It worked. I could not wait for Ṇẹṇẹ́,[10] as grandma was fondly called. Although we called our mother the same title, but with a different intonation on the last syllable. I was excited to do my part in making the place comfortable for Ṇẹṇẹ́, hence my mum's trick worked.

The summer holiday[11] had begun, so we all expected Ẹhi, my eldest brother, to be home for the two-month-long holiday. Ẹhi had moved to Benin, the capital city of my home state, Edo, about three years ago, to live with my aunty. *Sister,*[12] as we all called her, was my mum's elder sister. Strangely, her own children also addressed her by the same title. Sister had convinced my parents that secondary schools in Benin were far better than those in Lagos. We were all easily convinced, as my cousins were said to have aced all their *Waec,*[13] or so we heard.

Typically, chores were divided among children in many families in Nigeria. I hated doing the dishes. Nevertheless, I found an interesting way of enjoying it these days. I used my imagination to make the chores fun. The plates and spoons were a family, while the pots and spatula were their cousins, each dishwashing time was beach time. While the soap tablets were friendly dolphins and orcas, the lather they produced were the beach foam washed ashore by the ocean, represented by the water in the dishwashing basin. I was the lifeguard to pull them all out at the end of that chore.

"Ẹhi will miss out on hearing the stories told by Nẹnẹ. I wonder why he hasn't come for the holiday," I said to Uwa, my other brother, as we tidied the room.

"He's got exams to write, and Sister has

asked that he stay back and attend special holiday tutorials," Mum cut in. "Besides he's heard much of Nẹnẹ's stories on her last visit, so he's not really missing out on those," she continued.

"Why do my cousins call their mother Sister?" Uwa asked.

Mum was amused by the question, and she could not hold back her laugh as she answered.

"You know, it's kind of my fault... Poor kids, they got their bad habit from me. Back in the day, as a teenager, I lived with my sister, before her kids were born," she said

She told us she nurtured and spent more time with my cousins when they were very little than their mum ever did. They grew up hearing their mother being called Sister by her younger sister, and somehow they picked up the habit and never stopped, even into adulthood. Now everyone calls her Sister, including my other maternal cousins.

Mum often came in to help us fold the bedsheets and blankets. She taught us to work together as a team to get things done, by holding out the sheets at both ends and then coming together to have them neatly folded. An art we never mastered.

While we were at our chores, Uwa and I got into a conversation about the previous school term.

"Did Victor get his provisions back from the senior students?" I asked Uwa.

"Who is Victor and what did the seniors do to his provisions?" Mum interjected.

At this point, I could see the disappointment on Uwa's face, he never wanted Mum to know about some of the happenings in his boarding school hostel. I must have spoken a little too loud, enough for Mum to hear us.

"Tell me, who is Victor and what did the senior students do to him?" Mum probed further.

She dropped the cobweb duster in her hand and leaned forward to pay close attention to what Uwa had to say.

"He's my housemate," he reluctantly said.

"So? What did the senior boys do to him? What happened to his provisions?" Mum impatiently inquired.

In a bid to keep him less distracted, she sent me off to go check on my younger sisters, if they had awakened from sleep, but he only constantly stared at the floor and raised his head intermittently to look into my eye to show his disappointment; he didn't want Mum to know.

At this point, Mum knew it was only going to be futile trying to get words out of her second son. Uwa was different from me. He never spilt any word or information under pressure, so Mum knew not to probe further about Victor, she would wait for a more opportune time to mildly get him to talk.

She was always interested in what her kids were up to with their peers at school. On one occasion I told her about some comments my classmate Seun had made about her hair when she came to my school for a parent and teacher meeting.

Mum had very lovely long hair. She would comb it and just let it flow down to her shoulders, and when she walked, it swayed asymmetrically with her steps. You could not help but notice her well-arranged locks, as they formed slight curls at their tip. I could recognize her from 200 meters away. On the day of her visit to my school, I saw her through my class window.

My classroom was on the first floor of my school building. I sat just by the window facing east, overlooking the entire Afọnka Street.[14] It was a very interesting view. Every day I saw people and vehicles slowly moving on the untarred road, cars and pickup trucks going in and out of potholes filled with brown bodies of stagnant water. It was common to see women by the sidewalks, carrying on their heads,[15] trays filled with Ogi,[16] moulded into balls and wrapped in cellophane bags, calling out in loud voices to people to come buy their goods.

"Ẹ ra ogi ẹ po ẹko o,"[17] they would advertise.

There were also traders standing behind their wooden stands, selling loaves of bread on either side of the road, as they constantly tried to chase away the dogs that ran, hopped and barked around them in the morning sun. The district police station was to the north of the window, and a few times my classmates and I would watch as police forced criminals into their pickup vans in handcuffs. The second window facing east of the street overlooked *Mummy Tawa's* shop, the middle-aged woman who sold some of my favourite childhood snacks—Eekanna Gowan,[18] Balewa,[19] Kuli kuli,[20] Baba Dudu,[21] Goody Goody,[22] and Kokoro.[23] I had spotted Mum from a distance as I sat by the window, and I immediately beckoned to Seun.

"That's my Mum!"

"Who? The old woman getting off the bus?" he asked.

"What? My mum is not that old. It's the pretty woman with beautiful hair. Look at her in the white flowing maxi gown," I replied with pride.

"No way!" he reacted, looking thunderstruck. "I would have thought she was your elder sister, she's so young, and… b-b-beautiful. I like her hair in particular."

My reaction was mixed. A part of me felt happy about these compliments; at the same time, I thought Seun was too young to comment on her looks, it seemed somewhat disrespectful.

"How is it she looks so young and her hair is so beautiful, and her Cinderella dress as well?" he continued with fondness while stretching to get a clearer view as Mum neared the entrance gate and gradually went out of sight.

I shoved him off as his entire weight was on my stomach and his overly admiring her was irritating me. He had gone ahead to tell half of the class about "Harrison's young beautiful mum," and that angered me all the more; now every one of my classmates slyly walked past the headmaster's office, which was along the hallway leading to the toilet. They all feigned wanting to use the toilet just to get a peek of her. It was one of my most embarrassing days in school.

I got back home that day and in my almost regular fashion, left my backpack in the passage between the kitchen and living room. Today, before I got into that bad habit, my mum's piercing voice stopped me; it was as if the gripping sound clenched my hand, tightly holding the back.

"Do not drop that bag there, take it to the room," she authoritatively said.

I didn't know she was in the kitchen getting lunch ready, and as we rushed to tell her what went down at school, I stood by the door, taking in the aroma of beans and Dòdò[24] being served, and began telling her about my classmates' reaction to seeing her.

"Seun was surprised you were my mum," I said.

"Who's Seun and why was he surprised?" she retorted.

"He thought you were my sister," I continued, not answering her question. She was curious to know why two preteens would discuss such a topic.

"He didn't know you were my mum," I replied.

"Yeah, I heard you, but why did he think that?" she probed further.

"I don't know. I guess he feels you look quite young or something," I shrugged as I reached out to receive the plate of food she was handing me.

At this point, she seemed uninterested in my school talk and became distracted with serving lunch, asking me to go get my siblings to come for their meals. It seemed she already got her answers.

Chapter *Three*

ANTICIPATION

Although Nẹnẹ's arrival was going to be late in the evening, my anxiety was sky high. It was unbelievable she was showing up in a few hours. It was, for her, a road trip of about six hours. According to Mum, bus and coach stations were rare, and if there were any, they were in the big cities like Lagos where we lived. Nẹnẹ's village had none. I asked her how people made interstate travel; I wanted to know how Grandma was making it down to Lagos. I didn't think of air travel as an option, even though Dad used to use those a lot back in the day. Perhaps I thought only very rich people got on aeroplanes and I did not consider us that wealthy. She said few men were popularly known for being in the business of interstate taxi services. So, villagers would visit motor parks to book a spot and save seats with these men well ahead of their travel dates. They also provided their residential address details. On departure day, the taxi man would go to passengers' home to pick them up for the journey. Phones were not rampant, so every passenger had to be ready at the pre-agreed time. I used to imagine being on such a journey. Mum told me that it was very different from commuting within town, where you would see a lot of buildings and heavy traffic. On interstate motorways, on the other hand, you mostly saw vast land areas with vehicles driving at higher speed limits, tearing past forests and huge trees as their leaves and branches waved at drivers and passengers, and large cumulus clouds hovering above like halos.

I enjoyed getting on the bus with Mum when she went shopping. I remember a particular experience when I went to the food market at Ile Epo[25] with her. In my usual manner, whenever a bus arrived at the bus stop, I would quickly go ahead of her, just so I could pick an empty roll and sit by the window. I loved to hear the sound of the breeze clattering against the window frame. I would open the window wider than Mum wanted it. She didn't like what the wind did to her hair, it would cause it to either get into her eyes or mouth, I used to love watching how she constantly and stylishly used her index finger to flick some off her eyes and mouth. Occasionally she caught sight of me sticking an arm out to feel the rushing breeze, and whenever she caught me in the act, she strongly rebuked me. She had warned many times not to stick even a finger out the window of a moving vehicle. One time she told my siblings and me of a woman who had her hand wrenched by a messenger bike while she stuck her arm out of a moving bus. I never quite believed that story, it was horrid enough to get me cautioned whenever I was reminded of it though. Many Nigerian mothers used a lot of hyperboles just to set their kids straight, and my mum was no exception.

As our bus quickly moved past everything —trees, pedestrians, buildings along the way, in my adventurous mind, though, they were also quickly moving in the opposite direction. My favourite experience on road trips was imagining that we were in a racing competition with other vehicles. The sheer delight and disappointment I felt when we either overtook or were overtaken made it even more real. I remember one time, we struggled to beat a Volvo salon car. There was a lot of traffic that day, and our bus could not easily glide through, and the car kept evading us. I genuinely felt the driver was intentionally competing. We did eventually go past our *opponent,* and in childish ecstasy, I punched my fist in the air and shouted, "yeah!" to the surprise of my mum, who sat next to me. I liked to think that the driver of the Volvo saw me celebrating and would have probably felt disappointed while I gloated.

In those days, I hardly needed an alarm to wake me up. Mum had found a way to pass on her *early to bed, early to rise* habit to us. But even if I did oversleep, I would be woken up by either Dad's radio or the rising sun, because my window was to the northeast. I always loved to watch it rise, so I made sure to always wake up before it. I loved to see its golden rays pour through my window, leaving lines of shadows on the window frame on my wall, and because of the angle, these shadows took the shape of the pyramids of Giza. Well, at least, that was how I liked to imagine it.

Today, however, I was a little distracted. My mind was fixated on Nẹnẹ's arrival, and I still had a lot of my things to either evacuate or properly arrange to get the place ready for her. It was also on this day that I learned the background story and significance of my native name, "Ẹdeghọnghọn," often shortened as simply "Eghọnghọn."[26] I had a love for browsing through old pictures, so I had taken and kept an entire album from my dad's room. This fell off from the pile of clothes I was evacuating from my wardrobe, and a postcard fell out. I remember it was a picture of my father in a hospital bed, with the whole of his left leg in Plaster of Paris. I knew this was before I was born because I saw Uwa in the picture, who was just a toddler at the time, and he was three years older than I was. I knew this picture explained the limp in my dad's walk, but I had no idea whatsoever those events had a bearing on my naming. I always felt sad whenever I saw that picture.

"How long will it take you to get things cleared out? It's already midday, I bet Nẹnẹ́ is halfway through her journey now," Mum shouted from the corridor as she walked toward the room.

Her gradually approaching footsteps built the anticipation for the question I was about to ask her. She expected to see me scrambling to get things done as she walked in, instead, she found me sat and sombre. Her surprise mixed with concern as her eyes caught me staring at this picture that held, perhaps, one of the most tragic moments in the family's history. She dragged her feet gently toward me, I could hear the whooshing against the floor even though I sat with my back to her. When she came to standing before me, she asked if anything was the problem, to which I requested to know what exactly caused the accident and how long Dad spent in the hospital before being discharged.

She said his company's staff bus had run him over one morning while he stood at the daily rendezvous point. For some reason, the driver had not seen him waving and chasing down the bus. He got knocked over, with his legs run over by the wheels, leaving with him dislocated joints and broken bones from waist to femur to shin and all the way to his ankle.

"What has this got to do with my name

though?" I asked.

Mum said they thought he had completely lost his legs and ability to ever walk. He was in the hospital for months, with no recovery nor discharge day in sight. During this period, she was also pregnant with me, and the last trimester saw a great improvement in his condition, and he was nearer to recovery. With a smile full of emotions, Mum looked at me and revealed the connection with my name.

"He got fully discharged from the hospital on the day you were born, and we could finally go home. It was indeed a day of joy, hence your name," she said tearfully. "Your name means 'day of rejoicing.'"

At this point, I had started to get emotional too, and I struggled to hold back tears. I have kept a copy for myself to this day. Even though the relationship between my dad and I went on to become more and more unfriendly, this day struck a connection between him and my heart, an unconditional love for him.

Mum helped me get the last of my things either arranged or evacuated, and the room was set for Nẹnẹ. Constantly, I stared at the gate through the corridor window, hoping she was arriving soon. The afternoon sun usually came with occasional strong breezes in these parts, and at times they pushed the gate so hard that they made the bolts and locks jangle, creating a false alarm of my grandma's arrival. Normally the thrill and freedom that came with the long midyear school holiday meant more and more time for watching cartoons on television, but the anxious wait on this day took away all of that interest. I constantly imagined Nẹnẹ's journey—as the car approached ever closer, cutting through the wind as it ascended and descended the hilly Lagos-Benin motorways. I wondered if she was as eager to see me, to see all of us.

Chapter *Four*

THE ARRIVAL

Finally, in the early hours of the evening, a long honk was heard at the gate, and my instincts were not wrong this time. I jumped up from where I was sitting in the parlour and shouted to my mum.

"They're here!"

She responded with a smile as if to say, "yes, that's a familiar honk."

At this time, a sudden dilemma struck me. I didn't know if I should rush to the gate to welcome her or not. I was shy. My excitement and eagerness suddenly turned

Nẹnẹ́ in the early '90s

into unpleasant anxiety. I couldn't explain it. I also didn't want to act on my excitement as an overreaction and then not have her energy and enthusiasm match mine. So I decided to wait behind while my mum and siblings headed for the gate, and I just peeped from the window.

As they stepped out of the compound, all I could see were legs from beneath the gate, more like silhouettes of legs moving back and forth. From that distance, I could hear unintelligible voices, with obvious excitement in the air. Eventually, Mum and Uwa came in with a bag and luggage and then went out again. A few moments later, my mum and another woman moved toward the entrance while still standing on the outside, they seemed to be talking to someone and also handing something to them. I imagined this would have been them paying off the taxi driver, because a few seconds later I heard the sound of a car engine as the vehicle drove away past the gate entrance. The other woman then walked in with my sisters, both standing on either side of her, she had her arms around their shoulders. Surely this was my grandma, she obviously looked much older than my mum. Uwa and Mum helped with her things. He was struggling with his luggage, but rejected any help offered by Mum, he felt a sense of fulfilment helping this special guest. They all walked slowly toward the house, everyone obviously filled with cheer and laughter.

"Where is Eghọnghọn?" Nẹnẹ´ asked in our native language, Ẹsán.

To which Mum responded by yelling my name. I immediately got out of my hiding place and, in a very shy manner, rushed to go hug her. When she stopped to hug me,

I put my face down, as I was too shy and nervous. Nẹnẹ́ drew me tight to her bosom and rubbed her palm over my head, trying to get me to look at her.

"You're now so grown. You still recognize me, don't you? The last time I was here you were this tiny," she said while stooping and demonstrating with her hand a little over seven inches above the ground.

She tried to convince me to look at her, tilting my chin upward with her fingers, but I kept resisting. Eventually, Mum said to leave me alone.

"That's the way he is, he's just shy, at least for now. A few minutes from now he'll be all over you asking lots of questions. Give him time," she said.

The two women giggled, and we all went into the house.

In this part of the world, it was customary for anyone coming from their hometown, or at least from a very far distance to bring along lots of foodstuffs and snacks. Earlier in the year when Dad travelled for a week to see my other grandmother, his mum, he came with a bag full. This time it was Nẹnẹ's turn. The fruits from these parts were very organic and tasted very different, better, I would argue. According to Nẹnẹ, they were grown and harvested on domestic farms. I preferred these to the ones here in the city, which were grown for commercial purposes. Among my favourites were the Ube,[27] Agbálùmọ`.[28] She also brought along my favourite snack, Donkwa,[29] or Tanfili,[30] as it was popularly called in Lagos. Once we caught sight of the Tanfili, my siblings and I rushed for the bags like scavenger vultures around a carcass in the open desert. We only relaxed our scrambling after Nẹnẹ́ told us there was plenty to go round more than twice, that she even had extra in her personal purse. Interestingly— they were her favourite as well.

It was not long before Mum and Nẹnẹ́ began catching up, and doing so in Ẹ̀sán. Whatever they were saying became more and more unintelligible to us kids. We didn't really speak the language that much, we barely even understood it. My parents tried to teach us, but the influence of the local language, Yorùbá, was stronger. We tried to catch up, with that childish jealousy, frustration, and a scramble for attention. Something did not seem right! Somehow it had been registered in our minds that grandparents were mostly fond of their grandkids. So this felt wrong, very wrong. As Mum and Nẹnẹ́ laughed away and walked to the room that had been prepared,

I leaned against the old sewing machine that stood beside the window as I tried to make sense of whatever they were laughing about. I soon began fiddling with the balance wheel and pedal with my hands and right leg. Soon I tried to pull my full weight on the pedal. It had become so stiff due to lack of use and lubrication. I soon began enjoying the gradual rhythmic creaking sound of the spinning wheel, despite Mum's warning to stay away from the machine. As it spun and gained pace, the not-so-sturdy old machine tilted to its right, almost tipping over. At this point, Ṇẹṇẹ́ called out with a calm but piercing voice,

"Eghọnghọn! get off the machine. Did you not hear your mother?"

I immediately stopped and replied in the affirmative. She then walked toward me and pulled me to her bosom.

"You haven't been a naughty boy all this while, have you?" she inquired.

I shook my head in response. But my mum, who had now gone to the kitchen and heard her question, immediately countered, telling Nẹnẹ́ how I have constantly been restless and careless.

"He's either singing to himself in the dark or falling off a tree," she shouted.

By this time Mum had come back to the room and held my left arm up to reveal my wrist, which made me wince. I tried to hide my discomfort, but my mum immediately pointed to my face.

"See?! That face over there, it's as a result of this wrist. This boy nearly killed me, I thought he had lost an arm. He's not been a good boy o,[31] Nẹnẹ́."

"What happened?" Nẹnẹ́ inquired.

With no hesitation, my mum began narrating to her something I had done a year ago. I was not particularly proud of that incident, especially as it was being revealed to our special guest. Ironically though, there was an excitement and heroic feeling that I felt as Mum told of my exploits nonetheless.

Mum used to say I had an overly imaginative mind, that in my eyes everything in the world around had life, and somehow I found a way to communicate with them. She said I sometimes overthought things, and many times I acted out these thoughts—from re-enacting a movie or cartoon scene, to making origamis, and speaking with kitchen utensils, as if we were all part of some wild adventure or treasure hunt.

About a year ago, I had seen a barn funnel weaver crawl out of a hole in the bathroom door and my childish mind immediately thought itself being Peter Parker[32] in Spiderman. The little arachnid was desperate to get away from me, but I had other ideas, I imagined I could persuade him to inject some spider abilities into my bloodstream, just like in the movie. Every time I tried to hold the little fellow it hopped off, and because I didn't want to crush him whenever I got hold of him, I let it just crawl around the back of my hand, but it constantly spun its web and hung off my fingers upside down, a spectacle to my childish mind.

"Help me spin webs and glide the way you do," I whispered continually to him.

He seemed to have eventually heard and granted my childish plea, slowly crawling up to my hand and leaving a prickly sting on my wrist. I felt excitement rather than dread of possible pain, swelling, and nausea. Eagerly, I let it crawl away while I ran to the backyard to climb the eleven-foot fence around my compound. I helped myself by holding fast to the eleven-foot steel pole that stuck out of the concrete floor. The television antenna used to hang on it, before a heavy wind storm blew it off.

Now at the top of the wall, I smiled in accomplishment as I looked to shoot organic webs from my wrist, just like the movie superhero famously does. I should have pre-tested my *newly acquired powers* before jumping, but instead, I leapt off without any shred of doubt in my mind, stretching out my left hand to release my webs, which would stick to the house wall, allowing me to hang off it. I soon realized I did not become Spiderman. I landed awkwardly on my left hand and dislocated my wrist. It was my mum who, from the kitchen, heard my loud cry of anguish and rushed to pick me up off the ground to get my wounds tended to. I could tell from her face that she felt a rush of mixed emotions—fear, compassion, disappointment, and anger, and I could read the words, "This boy, you've done it again, you never listen, you'll put me in heartache. What do I do with you this time?" Even though the wound did heal, the scar never left, I still carry a faintly visible lump around the back of my wrist, and I feel a sharp pain in the area whenever I attempt to lift heavy objects with my left hand.

At the end of Mum's narration, Nẹnẹ́ pulled me and held me closer and gave a mild reprimand.

"You shouldn't be climbing walls and jumping off them, you know, right? If you don't promise me now you will stop, then all the goodies in store for you won't be revealed," Nẹnẹ́ whispered.

Hearing that threat was as scary as being left alone in the dark right after seeing a scary movie. The thought of seeing my entire hope and anticipation of night stories being dashed sent chills down my spine. Without hesitation, I made her the promise, anything to save my dream.

She pulled me closer into a tighter warm embrace and kissed me on the forehead. There was a soothing old lady scent that accompanied the strands of her gradually whitening hair. She had a constant smile on her face and she spoke with much poise and grace.

"Alright, Rose," she called to my mum, "these kids are tired and hungry, what's for dinner?"

Mum, who was already in the kitchen making dinner, replied, "Almost done, everything should be set on the table in a few minutes."

Before long, my siblings and I were carrying our bowls of food from the kitchen to the dining. It was the tradition that every child went to carry for themselves their meals from the kitchen. If an adult's meal was included, then as a sign of respect, you take theirs to them; this time though, Mum had both her mother's and hers in her hand.

A few moments after we had all sat down to eat, everyone had almost eaten halfway into their "Ẹba"[33] and Okra soup and I had barely started, just fiddling with a morsel and constantly dipping it in and out of my bowl of soup. Mum caught sight of me, gave me the familiar stern look, and I managed to swallow the morsel in my hand, accompanied by all the discomfort and distaste my face conjured. At this point, she got very angry, kissed her teeth, pushed her bowls aside, and shouted in a very strong voice,

"You have started again, haven't you? What..."

Nẹnẹ́ extended a hand to interrupt her by gently touching the back of her palm which was firmly rested on the dining table, and then turned to me.

"Why are you not eating, Eghọnghọn?" Nẹnẹ́ asked.

"He doesn't like *okwor soop*," Ẹse, my younger sister, responded in her babyish holophrases, trying to pronounce okra soup.

"Is that so, Eghọnghọn? Why, This is one of the best soups I've had in a long, long time," Nẹnẹ́ said.

"Nẹnẹ́, don't bother yourself, just eat your food so you don't choke, I'll handle this," Mum interjected.

She stood up from her seat and

interchanged her position with Ẹse's, who sat next to me on the left. This time I knew what was coming, and I definitely knew I was going to guzzle up every morsel on that plate in a few minutes. All she did was look me straight in the eye and tell me, in a very strong tone, "Now let me see you eating your food, and no scraps or crumbs left on that plate."

When my mum spoke that way, I understood what was coming if I ever disobeyed. Within a few minutes, my plate was squeaky clean. But Nẹnẹ́ had more things to tell me.

"Eghọnghọn do you know okra soup is the best? Do you know it is the soup of love and bond between families?" she said in a slow-paced tone.

My eyes beaming with curiosity, I looked at her and shook my head.

"Oh, I see your mum hasn't been teaching you lessons with the old tales of our people."

Yes! The moment was arriving, I was almost bursting into tears, the tales were about to begin. I went from one sombre kid to an uncontrollable ecstatic one. My dreams were coming true. It turned out that my siblings were getting the same idea.

"No, we've never heard such tales," Uwa immediately replied.

"Ah, Esther, you haven't been telling them?" Nẹnẹ́ turned to my mother.

In a coy manner, Mum responded, "Um... I have been singing the folk songs to them."

"Ah, Esther, you weren't even up to Uwa's age when I started with you," she smiled at her daughter while she playfully scolded her.

I could see they were having a real bonding time with this, lots of nostalgic emotions for my mum especially. It did feel weird to think of my mother as a child. In a child's mind, at least in mine, mums have always been mothers.

"Don't worry kids, tomorrow I shall tell you about Ojogbo Ẹlimi,"[34] Nẹnẹ́ said.

I naturally would have asked what Ojogbo Ẹlimi meant, but with the overwhelming excitement and anticipation, I didn't bother, there was a moonlight story coming up!

"It's getting late now; you kids are tired. You should go have your bath and rest up," Nẹnẹ́ encouraged.

All I remember was clearing the table of the plates along with my siblings, I was so tired I slept off without knowing when my father arrived from work that night. I did get awoken by his early morning routine though, he never missed a day.

Chapter *Five*

AWAKENING

Morning came very fast, but the night was definitely interesting. I had the most realistic dream ever. I was there, I was in the setting. It felt too real to be just a dream. I did not want it to end. They say dreams are figments of our imagination, experiences, and anticipation. As much as I wanted to remain in this imaginary world, I longed for the real deal, so I woke up!

The chickens never sounded this loud, the chirping and cooing of the sparrows and mourning doves felt closer than they ever had. The early morning sun never felt this friendly and healthy, I could swear I almost physically felt the vitamin D flowing into my bloodstream from the rays seeping through my window. Today I believed my science teacher's lessons on the morning sun's health benefits.

For me and my siblings, it was our happiest day yet, and we looked forward to the evening. We would usually want the days to last longer, because that meant more playtime. Nẹnẹ́ and Mum spent most of the day catching up. We would intrude once in a while, especially when any of us had a cause for complaint against the other as a result of mischief or rough play. Nẹnẹ́ was always quick to remind Uwa and me that we were the older ones and should treat our younger sisters fairly, but she also never failed to let the girls know they needed to respect their older brothers.

It was barely dusk, and I had started reminding Nẹnẹ́ of Ojogbo Ẹlimi. She smiled, and her responses were always cheerful.

"Don't worry, we have all evening, it's a long, long one," she reassured. "I hope you've got mats to spread outside, story times are sweeter in the cool of the night, under the moonlight."

Those words sent goose bumps all over my body.

As the day slowly darkened and the crickets started chirping, the owls hooting and the bats hovering around the Ikhimi[35] tree, my excitement knew no bounds. It was like the entire ecosystem in the compound was invited to this party.

We got ourselves ready on the mats and placed one of the kitchen stools in the centre, placing it against the wall so Nẹnẹ́ could rest her back while the evening lasted. Tonight, we had dinner outside on the mats. It was my favourite soup, Ọgbọnọ,[36] and we had it with Pounded Yam.[37] Just as Mum was serving the meals, Nẹnẹ́started singing.

Emi iye mwen ọna emi o

Aré a khọlọ ọna emi o[38]

She raised her elbows while moving them rhythmically along with her song.

"What does that song mean, Nẹnẹ?" I asked with suspenseful eyes.

"It's one of the songs in the story I'm about to tell you, and it is also about you and your mother. Be patient, my child, and you'll understand everything as we delve into the world of wonders in the very ancient land far, far away, when animals, spirits, and humans very much interacted with each other," she replied with a smile on her face.

This time our eyes lit up and we had to pause eating for about ten minutes, the starchy pounded yam leaving dried hard crumbs on our hands. Mum interjected and interrupted.

"Ah ah, Nẹnẹ́, let them finish up first, there's enough time."

Nẹnẹ́ acquiesced, and we hurriedly finished our food.

Part Two

Chapter *Six*

A LAND FAR, FAR AWAY

❝In a land far, far away, there lived a king, Ojiso, along with his wives**❞** were Nẹnẹ's opening words for her story.

It was finally time. By now the evening had become quieter. The only sounds we could hear were the gentle night breeze that beat our earlobes and the chickens as they slowly coop chattered. The moon had come out in its full radiance, with the clouds occasionally moving across it. I took one brief moment to take in the environment, noticing the owl had left the Ikhimi tree to come settle on the tip of the rooftop, and the bats had stopped hovering, but I could not tell where they had gone. It was like these friends of mine had also calmed down, ready to hear the thrilling story, and those opening words transported me into my imagined setting of the story.

In my mind, I pictured a village square, which was located adjacent to, but separated from the main residential houses, and hosted a number of activities including town hall meetings, and games, and other ceremonies. And overlooking all of these on the west was a two-storey mansion, which was the king's palace.

"Wives? Or do you mean to say 'wife,' Nẹnẹ?" I interrupted, as the concept of polygamy, until that moment, was unclear to me.

"Wives, my dear," she replied. "In those days, many kings had more than one wife.

And Ojiso had seven."

Nẹnẹ́ continued her story...

"Now, all of these wives except the youngest had born him children. However, the king was not happy, there was doubt and a lack of surety over the security of his line and the dream of a lasting dynasty, for he had no male child. Ojiso sought the intervention of the oracle, and he was advised to prepare a simple bowl of Ahà for all seven wives."

"What's Ahà, Nẹnẹ́?" I curiously asked.

"I don't know how to properly say it in English. I can describe it though. It is mashed yam mixed with palm oil, a bit of ground chilli, and salt. There are other ingredients native to our tribe, but I don't know their English words," she replied. "Anyway, back to the story. Try not to interrupt again, just follow with your mind."

The king was to add a secret ingredient to the Ahà—a seed of alligator pepper, just one. He was to stir it in the food and make sure it was not visible to the wives. Whichever wife who inadvertently picked and ate the seed was to bear a son.

The king had a favourite among his wives, called Anọhẹn, but everyone called her "Amẹbọ´"[39] because she was seen as not only his beloved but also his informant on all happenings in the house. Everyone, including the king, expected that she ate the fertility seed, but the oracle warned that Ojiso have no hand in it or else there will be dire consequences.

The last among the wives was an orphan who was much hated by the other wives. Her name was Uhumu. She was mistreated for her shyness and poor family background. Even the king was not so fond of her and wished she was not the choice of the gods to bear him an heir.

The day arrived for all seven wives to have the meal. They were all expected to eat from one bowl, and as usual, the last wife was bullied and pushed away from partaking in the course.

"You have no place here. We can't have you dip your filthy hand in the same bowl with us. Besides, no one wants you to bear the king's son."

Shamed and dejected, she sat at a distance in the room corner and watched them all eat the Ahà, and all she could do was watch and weep. Eventually, the other wives mockingly asked her to come feed from the scraps.

"Here! This is what you deserve. At least let it be known that we gave you part of the meal," they said.

"Did you think you ever stood a chance to bear a son?" Anọhẹn scoffed.

Without any hesitation, she reached for the bowl and ate the remnant with hope, hope that the seed was somehow still in the bowl. Suddenly she began screaming.

"My mouth, oh! Oh, my mouth!"

Everyone rushed to see what was happening, many thought she was either crazy or simply seeking attention.

"It's so hot, what pepper or chilli was used in the preparation of this meal? Oh, I need water. It's too hot, it's too hot," she kept screaming

At this point, they all realized she had eaten the alligator pepper seed, for this species of pepper was very hot, even a single seed of it. Devastated and desperate, the six other wives rushed to her and insisted she spat in their mouths, with the hope that she had not swallowed it. It was too late however, everything was already in her stomach. Word got to the king, but all he felt was mixed feelings. On the one hand, delight that he would eventually have an heir, on the other, disappointment that it was not going to be by his favourite, Anọhẹn, or at least any other person but the last wife.

Months gradually rolled by and the women neared their delivery. As it was customary in those days, the king was never to see eye to eye with his son, so all seven women were sent out to their families to have their babies.

The women set out for their respective family houses. With no family or home to return to, Uhumu begged to go with the rest, but none of them agreed to have her in their company.

As the other women walked on, she followed behind from a distance. Slowly, they approached the outskirts of the village, at the crossroads between the border river and the so-called forest of no return. Again, the orphaned woman begged to join their company, but they kept casting her off.

"Bad luck has always followed you, everywhere you go you bring bad luck. Go into the bush, into the forest where your kind are."

Chapter *Seven*

THE UNKNOWN

With fear in her heart and tears in her eyes, Uhumu slowly walked into the forest of no return. It was fabled that this forest was home to all kinds of spirits and anthropomorphic animals. No one ever dared to go into it, even the bravest of hunters and magic priests. It was told that many years ago the spirits of the forest once cohabited with humans, until they were betrayed, so the spirits left to live in isolation in the forest. No one knows to this day what crime exactly was committed or who the perpetrator was.

The most revered and feared of the forest

creatures was Ojogbo Ẹlimi, the spirit with seven heads. It was believed that he had killed many lost humans who had wandered into the forest. He took no prisoners.

Uhumu bore all of this in mind as she slowly made her way further, feet shaking, heart racing faster than normal, her lips quivering as though she was uttering words, if she did at all, they were gibberish born of terror.

As she delved deeper into the forest, it became quieter and quieter, it seemed like no one or nothing lived in it, until she arrived at a misty valley and caught sight of a plume of smoke rising in the distance. By now she was very hungry, so she decided to go down to the valley to find the source of the smoke and see if she could find food. When she had walked a distance at the bottom of the valley, she found a hut made of mud walls, with its roof thatched with palm leaves and branches.

"I would die here anyway, either by a wild beast or spirit or hunger, I better take my chances and see if whoever lives there has some food."

Uhumu slowly tiptoed into the hut as her eyes roved about the entire place. She couldn't reconcile the size of the interior with the exterior. Inside, the hut was as large as a mansion, the size of twenty huts put together. She felt her eyes were playing tricks on her due to exhaustion. So, she went out and looked again and then came back in. It was the same—the size of a hut outside but a mansion inside. She became very afraid, as she realized she was in the home of a spirit. She mustered the last of the courage in her and called out for anyone home.

"Hello! Is anybody home? I come in peace. I have travelled for days from the land of men, and I just need a place to rest my head and little food for my stomach, I'm dying." Her voice slowly drifted off as she continued losing strength.

She kept uttering those words, but no one answered. It seemed there was no one home. Only a fire flickering in the fire hearth with an earthen pot hanging above it. The house looked quite untidy, so Uhumu set to clean up and make everything well arranged.

"I'm going to check around for food, I'll eat and then have this whole place tidied up. Perhaps when the householder returns, he would spare me for doing their chores," she assured herself.

The house itself was filled with the aroma of mushroom soup, which was coming from the pot. Uhumu helped herself with a bowl full, after which she swept, dusted, and mopped the entire house. She made sure she arranged everything that seemed out of place until everywhere was squeaky clean. After all this work, she felt very tired and fell asleep.

The day slowly turned into dusk, and dusk to night, and the owner of the house began returning to their hut. Immediately they got to the doorpost, he stopped and sniffed very loudly.

"I smell a human," he said.

He had returned with seven bundles of firewood. Each bundle contained ten logs, and he carried each bundle on each of his seven heads. He was Ojogbo Ẹlimi.

Uhumu was so deep in sleep that she did not hear him walk into the house or when he spoke. But as soon as he began dropping the firewood, one by one, the loud banging sound as they hit the ground woke her up, and she became struck with fear. She crawled beneath a large table that was hidden in a shadow. She tried very hard to hold her breath as she watched the approaching feet of the Ojogbo Ẹlimi, they were enormous, like those of seven men combined. Each of them had seven toes. He walked back and forth, slowly calling out to the intruder in his house.

"Come out, come out, little fly. You have dared to come into the home of Ojogbo Ẹlimi the mighty. I am the monster with seven heads. There is no hiding place for you. My fourteen eyes see every angle, every corner of this house. There is no hiding place for you, there is no shadow under which you can hide or block my vision."

At this point, Uhumu began snivelling, as she could not control herself, for fear had overtaken her. While she was trying to hold her breath, Ojogbo Ẹlimi stuck one of his heads under the table.

"Boom! There you are," he said.

Uhumu cowered in fear and began to weep. Ojogbo Ẹlimi dragged her out by her foot, and asked her how she had gotten to the hut and what she was doing here.

"Wait, you're from the king's palace, one of his wives sent to bear his son. Oooh, I have ears, I know things. You're my prisoner now!" he said.

Ojogbo Ẹlimi roared as she begged for his mercy, but each time she tried to speak and plead her case, he constantly shut her up. Even though he spared her life, he had her tethered, albeit with long cords, enough for her to reach around the house. She did his daily chores, and he let her take food from the earthen pot whenever she wanted.

Chapter *Eight*

PRISONER

Days turned to weeks and weeks into months, and the day came for her to deliver her child. He had her blindfolded while he delivered her of the baby—a boy! Ojogbo Ẹlimi had used his magic to prevent her from hearing the infant's cry while he replaced it with an Osukhamẹdin[40] from a palm tree, swaddled in cloths. He then hid the baby away from her and took it to a secret room where he had a big pot that was constantly sat in a fire hearth, he unwrapped it and placed it inside to cook along with whatever was in it.

"Here, this is your baby! Here's what you've delivered, no wonder you're much hated by the entire palace," he said as he took off the blindfold and handed the Osukhamẹdin to her.

Uhumu wept bitterly every day, as she was forced by the monster to nurture this lifeless stock.

"Mother Nature must hate me; the gods certainly have placed a curse on me. What more is the value of my life? Am I not better off dead?" she would say every day.

Every time she said this, he would reply her, saying, "You will not die; you must nurture this baby till it grows."

"But how do I do this? It is lifeless!" she said to him.

"Well, it is your baby. You delivered it, you must not throw it away, for on the day that you do, I shall kill you," he retorted.

He then gave her a daily assignment—she was to go into the secret room blindfolded every morning to drop all sorts of herbs and vegetables in the pot where he had placed the baby. He strongly warned her that if she ever opened her eyes to see the room or look into the pot he would kill her.

"Even when I'm not in the house, I see what you're up to, so do not test me," he boasted.

Uhumu was too scared to disobey the monster, and she continued in this routine daily until the day the King's wives were to return to the palace. Three and a half years had passed since she saw the plume of smoke rising from the distance. During all of this time, Ojogbo Ẹlimi had become unusually nice to her—making sure she lacked nothing, not food or clothing. Although

he revealed nothing about her baby to her
or what he had done with it.

Chapter *Nine*

THE REVEAL

Ojogbo Ẹlimi had promised to let Uhumu leave for the palace when it was time for the women to return, so on the morning, he took it upon himself to get her all packed and ready for the journey, after which he called her into the room where the pot was.

"Come in, come take your child. I have him already swaddled, nice and warm, all ready for your departure," he said.

She walked in slowly, weeping with quivering lips, hands shaking as she tried to shut the door behind, her head faced down in grief and fear as she expected him to hand her the Osukhamẹdin.

"Here's your baby," he said with a very soft tone.

As she received it from him, her hands dropped, as this "baby" was unusually heavier than what she had nurtured for three years. Also, she felt it wriggle briefly. She could not believe her eyes as she saw a live baby, upon taking off her blindfold. Suddenly her tears of sorrow became those of joy, her heart became light, her face brightened as she pulled him closer to her chest and felt his beating heart.

All these years, Ojogbo Ẹlimi had been secretly nurturing the real baby to health and strength. He wasn't in the pot to be tortured or left to die. The pot contained a magic potion, and the herbs Uhumu threw into it were charms, concoctions that made him stronger and indestructible every day.

"This is really my baby, is it?" she cautiously asked.

"Yes, it is. It has always been. That's your strong and beautiful baby boy," again with an even softer tone, he replied.

Uhumu couldn't help but gush with gratitude while still tearing up in joy. She became hysterical. She was over the moon.

Ojogbo Ẹlimi now told her how he had taken the child at his birth and had been preparing him in the magic pot. He revealed to her that all the items she routinely dropped in the pot were the charms and herbs needed to make the boy strong and resistant to any ordeal or harm. The seven-headed monster had ensured Uhumu went in daily to the room of magic potion, not only to drop charms and herbs, but also that the baby felt and familiarized with his mother's presence.

"He has known you from birth, he will never be deceived nor cajoled into leaving you. No charm nor falsehood will sway him away," he assured her.

"You share a special bond. Now be on your way, your fellow wives are already on their way, you should meet them halfway, by the riverbank. Be very careful, as they will be filled with much envy," he warned her.

Uhumu set out to walk through the forest path leading toward the village where the king awaited his son and heir to the throne. This time she walked with so much confidence and hope, not fearing the quiet and misty forest. Somehow, she felt Ojogbo Elimi watched over her and would protect her against any sudden danger. Her heart was set on the palace and the possible change in her circumstances as the mother of the king's heir. Even the hooting sound of distant owls and flapping wings of vampire bats hovering over her was not a scare this time. Due to her ecstasy, she could have sworn she saw the trees lower their branches and leaves, bowing to her as the new queen mother. As she approached the end of the forest, and as the beams of light from the sun hit her face, she felt new and refreshed as she paused and took a last glance at the forest, ironically, in gratitude.

Chapter *Ten*

"ONE OF US"

As she strode on the path leading to the village, Uhumu could hear the voices of her co-wives from a distance, and they got louder as she gradually approached with slower steps and mixed feelings. Surely these women still hated her and were still angry that she had swallowed the alligator pepper seed, each of them bore in mind that Uhumu was the potential mother of the king's son. Although they also hoped she had perished in the forest of the spirits. The women had stopped to have their bath by the river on the border of the village, each had safely entrusted their baby girls to the hands of their accompanying maidservants. Immediately they caught sight of Uhumu, all chatting and giggling stopped, and there suddenly was an awkward silence that enveloped the entire area. These senior wives all stood upright, some with hands akimbo, others with folded arms as they stared at the timid and lowly Uhumu who approached with caution.

Suddenly Amẹbọ́ spoke up.

"What have you delivered? Pray, show us," she asked.

With reluctance, Uhumu tilted her swaddled infant forward to reveal his face.

"It's a boy," she said softly.

"Oh, so you did indeed swallow the magic seed," another wife said.

"Now the king will finally love you more than he does us. Now you may as well take my husband from me and assume my position," the first wife said.

At this, Amẹbọ'leaned forward to address all the women.

"The king is still our husband, and Uhumu our sister, at least we are all stepmothers to her son, and she, to our daughters. We can't continue to treat her as though she isn't one of us," she said.

The other women affirmed in unity their support of Amẹbọ's statement. They then each approached Uhumu and hugged her, each paying homage to the baby in her arms. At last, they convinced her to come to join in having a bath.

"We wouldn't want to go into the village square and certainly not the palace looking scruffy and dusty after trekking miles from our individual hometowns," Amẹbọ'said.

Uhumu, who had become more relaxed, now handed her baby to one of the maidservants as she made her way to join the other women for a bath. As soon as she was in the body of water, one of the other wives immediately rushed out to grab the baby boy from the maidservant.

"If we are not having the king's son, then over our dead bodies will you, Uhumu, an ordinary slave girl do," she screamed, and the other wives shouted in agreement.

The woman with the baby then threw him into the middle of the river, much to Uhumu's shock and horror. She had been tricked.

For once she thought she had been accepted as part of the family. She thought she finally could make the palace her home. She had failed to heed Ojogbo Elimi's warning. She wept and rolled on the riverbank, while the other women packed up and left. As they walked on toward the palace, Amẹbọ́ stopped and looked back with a malicious smirk, driving further into Uhumu's heart the stabbing agony she was feeling. Uhumu cried even louder, plunging into the edge of the shores of the river and calling to the spirits for help. She could not swim, so she could not dive in to rescue her son. She knelt by the river bank and wept bitterly, tears pouring endlessly from her eyes and nose.

"My baby, my child!! What have I done? How I've failed you. I should have known. I should have protected you," she wailed loudly, rolling and turning on the wet river shore.

Finally, she picked herself up from the ground to leave for the village.

Covered in mud, she dragged herself toward the palace. Pain and grief had blinded her from any embarrassment her appearance may have caused as she moved between a gathering crowd. She knew no one would believe her story; not the villagers, even worse, not the king.

Chapter *Eleven*

STRANGE VOICE

The day came for all seven wives to present their babies. All the wives, including Amẹbọ́, gathered in a room to get themselves and their children dressed up to approach the king at his throne. Now, because of what had transpired at the river, they all warned Uhumu not to speak of it. She herself knew the king would not even believe whatever she said, being his least favourite.

Meanwhile, on the same day of the presentation, a palm-wine tapper named Odigie had gone out on his daily routine of harvesting wine from the numerous palm trees on the outskirts of the village. Today he went up a palm tree just by the river into which Ọnaiwu[41] had been thrown and left to die. While he was up on the tree, with his belt firmly fastened around, getting his wine jar and hose out, he suddenly began hearing a voice singing. At first, he did not pay attention to it, as he thought it came from a village passer-by. However, the singing got louder, and the source seemed nearer than expected. As he looked down to pay closer attention, the voice seemed to be emanating from the body of water beneath.

Bewildered and anxious, he paid closer attention to the words of the song. They were strange and revealing. They went thus:

Ojiso is my father

Uhumu is my mother

Anọhẹn the Amẹbọ wished me dead and

threw me into the river

*But I am not dead, the gods have shown
me mercy and preserved me alive*

Alas, it was Ọnaiwu, Uhumu's son, who
was singing. Ojogbo Ẹlimi's charms had
kept him alive. Odigie could not believe his
ears. Troubled, he slid down the tree and
ran straight for the king's palace. Back at
the palace, the king was rueing his ill luck.
The wives had all presented their babies, and
still no heir. At the same time, the palm wine
tapper ran to approach the palace backyard
guards, breathing heavily and asking for an
audience with the king in private. While
Odigie was being deterred, the king saw the
scuffle through the window of his chamber
and asked that he be allowed into the
palace's inner chamber. Ojiso granted him
an audience and Odigie related everything he
heard at the riverbank, he revealed the exact

wordings of the song, much to the king's astonishment. Upon hearing everything narrated, Ojiso quickly ordered three of his guards to accompany Odigie to the river to confirm the story. He ordered them to not return without the boy if the whole story turned out to be true. The king, meanwhile, kept everything from all his wives, including Uhumu, and instructed everyone privy to the matter to do the same.

Very early the next morning, about the usual time Odigie would go into the bush for his wine harvesting, all four messengers from the king set out for the river. They had all agreed that the three guards will hide between the bush while Odigie climbed up the tree as if tapping wine. They did not want to do anything that would prevent the child from singing, perhaps unfamiliar faces may seem a red flag, and he took to defence.

Not long after the palm wine tapper had climbed up the tree, Ọnaiwu began singing. He repeated the same words as on the first day and kept repeating them loudly.

Ojiso is my father

Uhumu is my mother

Anọhẹn the Amẹbọ́ wished me dead and threw me into the river

But I am not dead, the gods have shown me mercy and preserved me alive

This time Odigie slowly climbed down and approached the riverbank. He began singing back to the child.

My name is Odigie

I am a palm wine tapper

I have heard your call

I have heard your cry

Ojiso has sent me to fetch you

Here, the king's guards have accompanied me to bring his son home

You are the king's son, the future king

At the end of Odigie's song, ripples and bubbles started forming and moving toward the river shores, and gradually Ọnaiwu emerged from the water. The men who had hidden behind the bush came out and slowly approached too, they brought blankets, clothes, jewellery, and ornaments befitting a prince. He was so handsome. His hair was long. His brown eyes glowing with sheen. They bathed the child and had him all dressed up and looking like royalty, ready for the palace.

Odigie and the guards secretly brought Ọnaiwu to Ojiso's private chambers. He was kept a secret for three days until the king was ready to reveal him to the entire village. Still in doubt about the boy's real mother,

Ojiso plotted a move. He asked all seven wives to prepare their very best dishes for an exhibition in front of the entire village. Each mother was to sit behind her meal and have their children walk up to eat at their feet. Although the women wondered why such a feast was being put together and to what end, they all rushed to get their food ingredients and got busy in the kitchen. The six wives took all that was made available by the palace and left only the scraps for Uhumu. Discouraged and sad that she had no child to present for the exhibition, the lowly woman put together what she could gather from the kitchen's floor and got ready for the feast.

Chapter *Twelve*

REUNION

As the king's wives lined up with their wonderfully garnished foods, they constantly made fun of Uhumu's, as it did not look so pleasant. Anọhẹn and some others even kept knocking it around with their feet.

"What kind of thing is this? It looks like garbage. Who is ever going to eat this poison?" they said.

The women finally called out to their children, and each daughter went to eat at her mother's corner. Uhumu sat alone, weeping and feeling dejected that she had no child coming to eat her food.

The king then asked his guards to bring Ọnaiwu to him. He revealed the boy to the crowd and asked him to go eat his mother's food. Everyone was surprised and wondered who the boy was and who was his mother. The senior wives all looked on with astonishment as they recognized the boy, although he was all grown now. Uhumu could not believe her eyes, it was her son, he was alive. She had become reinvigorated with pride and happiness as she uncontrollably waited for him to come toward her, she cried and wept with joy. The boy then walked on along the aisle where the women lined up with their dishes. He stopped at each woman's corner and sang for a few minutes before he moved on to the next.

My mother's food

My mother's food

This is not my mother's food

This cannot be my mother's food

He kept singing this way as he stopped by each woman's food, before moving on until he finally got to Uhumu and began singing.

My mother's food

My mother's food

Yes, this is my mother's food

Even if it doesn't look pleasant

Even if it is made out of scraps

This is my mother's food

The boy then sat and ate all of his mother's food and left nothing to spare, after which he hugged her and they both cried for a while, got up, and walked toward the king. Ojiso then had Odigie narrate everything that had happened before the entire village. Anọhẹn and her cohorts felt deep shame and fear, fear that the king would feel infuriated and may take drastic actions against them. The king became angry and chased away the other women. He now became more endeared to Uhumu. He also installed her as queen, and they lived happily ever after.

Part Three

Chapter *Thirteen*

MIDNIGHT MOON

"Wow! Grandma, that was a riveting story! I am happy how things turned out for Uhumu in the end. But what about Odigie, did the king reward him in any way?"
I asked, my eyes lit up with concern and a feeling of fondness.

"There has never been a mention of it in the story, in the many times it has been told," My mother cut in. "Or, Nẹnẹ́, is there some later part you never told us?"

Nẹnẹ́ shifted her gaze from my mum to me with a smile on her face, as if wanting to extend the story.

"Well, Odigie was a good man, wasn't he? Any good king would have rewarded such a person," Nẹnẹ́ answered. "And he was trustworthy as well, so that would come with some good ending," she assured me.

"Yes, yes! So he was rewarded then!" I said, trying to convince myself. "What about the other women, where did they go, and what happened to their daughters? Did the king send them away with their mothers?" I inquired. "They were innocent, right?"

"Of course they were," Nẹnẹ́ replied reassuringly. "Ojiso would want his princesses around him. He would want all his children to live together and experience the joys of having siblings around while growing up."

At this time my siblings had fallen asleep while the story was being told, and my mum was trying to get us all in to go sleep for the night.

"Alright, that's enough story time and questions for the night, we will continue another day," she said.

I could not help but slip in another question though.

"Do you think those women went back to their parents' houses or they went to live on their own within the village?" I asked Nẹnẹ.

"My dear son, don't worry about what happened after the story's end," she responded. "Focus on all you've heard and learned from the story. Was there any moral lesson for you?"

"Sure, Nẹnẹ. I never want to be proud and jealous like Anọhẹn. Also, goodness always has its reward," I said.

"That's correct, my boy, never forget those lessons," she replied.

Now she began smiling, as if being cheeky,

and said, "Also you should eat your mother's food *Even if it doesn't look pleasant*. Always remember that," she said, nodding her head and patting me on the shoulder.

"Yes, Ṇẹnẹ́," I replied. My curios mind quickly switching to yet another question brewing in my head.

Before I could ask, however, Mum cut in, she knew me too well that the questions will never end, and for her, it had become too late to still be outside. The weather was getting colder, and as always, she was worried about the mosquitoes. Ṇẹnẹ́ finally got up from the stool while she adjusted the wrapper[42] around her waist which had become loose. I quickly rushed to carry the stool from beneath her, to go along with into the house. It was the right and respectful thing to do, but also my mum would have had words for me if I had left Grandma alone to help herself with the little furniture.

"Thank you, my son," Nẹnẹ́said, with a grin on her face.

I felt so proud of myself as she pulled me closer, putting her arms around my shoulder and leaning closer, stooping lower to my ear she asked with a whisper, "What was it you were going to ask me? Do make it the last one though, before your mum catches us." She was smiling and giving a side-eye as if watching and hiding from Mum.

This felt so nice. It felt like we were a team, bonding so well and effectively. I could feel her love and protection.

"Are there more stories like this one you've told us? And will you be telling them tomorrow also?" I smiled and whispered back.

"Ah, yes, my son!" she replied. "Many more. I am sure I wouldn't be able to tell them all before I leave for the village. But don't worry, we will have a wonderful time together. But now the night is well along. I need to go have my rest. An old woman needs her rest. Good night, my son."

She kissed me on my forehead and went into the house while I stood with the stool in my hand. It was like her reassuring words about the fun times ahead catapulted me into a world of an unending chain of repeated fantasy tales. As I stood there and gazed into the darkness-filled compound, my imagination went wild, and the entire compound had become the village square in the Ojogbo Elimi tale. I turned to take a look at the garden on the side, with the crickets chirping from the dirt of fallen dried up leaves gathered around the plantain trees. I felt like I was staring at Ojogbo Elimi's hut, the branches moving with the wind

seeming like his seven heads. I had created an imaginary, gigantic size of the monster. It was like I was seeing a frightening, yet exciting vision.

I stood still, caught in my trance, my arms beginning to strain, I had forgotten I held Nẹnẹ's stool, its weight finally knocked me back to reality, my muscles stiffening as the breeze got cooler, forcing me into a brief shiver. I hurried to roll up the mat and get ready to retire for the night.

As I went through the door and made way for the room through the corridor, I could not help but notice the full moon's penetrating rays through the window, its silver lines drew a last gaze from me, and I could not wait for the next night, in this beautiful utopian setting of mine, caught in a world of imagination as I am sat at Nẹnẹ's feet under the bright moonlight. It was how

I wished all my nights would be. This was the perfect night, this was the ideal holiday for a child.

About The Author

Harrison is a creative artist with a strong passion for arts and culture. He is a graduate of English and Literature from the University of Benin, where he was also an actor for the department's association Playhouse- *ELSA Playhouse*, a theatre group known for staging plays across Benin City, Nigeria. Although he has gone on to explore career fields such as Banking and Information Technology, he has stayed true to his original passion. In recent times, he has launched an initiative to promote African creativity in arts and culture internationally.

Endnotes

1. Spiderman: Superhero character appearing in American cartoons and movies with the same title. He develops special powers, such as great strength and the ability to cling to surfaces, after being bitten by a radioactive spider.

2. Ayò Ọlọ́pọ́n: Board game indigenous to the Yorùbá people of south-western Nigeria and is widely played in most parts of the country. The two elements being 'Ayò' (Game) 'Ọlọ́pọ́n' (Intellectual) simply means "Game of Intellectuals."

3. Plantain: Also called Cooking banana. It is a staple in Nigeria, some other parts of Africa, the Caribbean, Central America, and parts of South America and South Asia. Unlike the regular bananas that are eaten raw, plantains

are usually cooked or otherwise processed before they are eaten.

4. Efirin: Also called 'Ewe Efirin.' It means "scent leaf" in Yorùbá. It is a tropical species of vegetables used in meals and is widely noted for its strong scent, nutritional and medicinal value.

5. Here the phrase "matriarch and patriarch" is used to express how the persona views and personalizes the animals- being organized within a system and descended from a family or clan head, as humans would.

6. "Alpha" and "Omega" are the first and last letters of the Greek alphabet. They are used in Christianity to illustrate God's infiniteness, hence being creator and all powerful. The persona here sees himself as such, within the world he's created in his mind.

7. Voice of America (VOA): The state-owned international radio broadcaster of the United States of America. It is primarily listened to by non-American audience. It was very popular in the '90s in Nigeria.

8. Don Williams: Popular American country music singer.

9. A line from Don Williams' song titled "You're My Best Friend", recorded in 1974 and released in 1975.

10. Nẹnẹ́: Ẹ̀sán word for Mother. Most native speakers also use it to refer to grandmothers, but with a higher tone on the last ẹ́. For mother, the diacritic would usually point downward to the right, like so, ẹ̀.

11. Summer holiday referred to the long midyear school holiday. Though there is no summer weather season in Nigeria, the term

is use that way, because the period coincides with those of Europe and America.

12. Sister: Popularly used in Nigeria as a title to show respect (rather than for a female sibling) to older female siblings and aunties.

13. Waec: Widely pronounced as an acronym—'*Wah-yek*', meaning West African Examination Council and is colloquially used to refer to the Senior Secondary (School) Certificate Examination. It is the equivalent of the UK's General Certificate of Secondary Education (GCSE).

14. Afọnka Street: A popular street in the persona's neighbourhood. Notable for its police station and officers.

15. Head porterage was a common practice in many rural neighbourhoods among street sellers and hawkers. With many cities

becoming more urbanized, the practice has been largely banned.

16. Ogi: Popular street food from Nigeria, made from fermented cereal such as maize, sorghum, or millet. When prepared it usually takes the form of pap.

17. A Yorùbá sentence which translates into "buy Ogi and make pap." It was a regular chant by hawkers of Ogi in many south-western neighbourhoods in Nigeria.

18. Ekanna Gowan: Cone shaped candy, made from molten sugar. Named after a Nigerian military ruler in the '60s, Yakubu Gowan. Ekanna, is the Yorùbá word for fingernail.

19. Balewa: Candy made with sugar, water and mint. Also named after Nigeria's first prime minister, Abubakar Tafawa Balewa.

20. Kuli kuli: West African crispy snack

primarily made from peanuts paste.

21. Baba Dudu: Hard dark brown coconut candy, made by boiling coconut milk down with sugar till it darkens and then moulded into round or oval balls. The two elements being '*Baba*' (father or old man) and '*Dudu*' (Black) translates to Blackman.

22. Goody Goody was a chocolate candy sold across Nigeria in the '90s. Kids loved it for its creamy taste.

23. Kokoro: A common snack in Nigeria made from maize flour paste mixed with sugar and cassava or yam flour and deep-fried.

24. Dòdò: Yorùbá word for deep fried plantain.

25. Ile Epo: A popular market in Lagos, Nigeria. The name is gotten from the fuel station located at the bus stop leading to the market. 'Ile' and 'Epo' are the Yorùbá

words for House and Oil (in this case petrol) respectively. Petrol stations are referred to as petrol houses.

26. Eghọnghọn: Ẹsán word for Happiness. In most cases it is the contraction of the name 'Ẹdeghọnghọn', which means "Day of Happiness".

27. Ube: Igbo word for the fruit, African pear. It is native to west Africa and largely found in south-eastern Nigeria.

28. Agbálùmọ̀: Yorùbá word for the African star apple. A fruit commonly found throughout tropical Africa.

29. Donkwa: Street snack made from roasted corn and peanuts. The word Donkwa is of Hausa origin, an ethnic group native to west Africa, with majority population in northern Nigeria.

30. Tanfili: Yorùbá equivalent of Donkwa.

31. O: Pronounced '*Oh*'. Nigerian exclamatory word used ubiquitously at the end of sentences to connote many ideas. It can be the answer to a call. It can be used in agreement. It can also be used to reiterate a point.

32. Peter Parker: The protagonist in the American superhero movie 'Spiderman.' He becomes Spiderman after being bitten by a radioactive spider.

33. Ẹba: Popular west African food made from cooked dried cassava flour.

34. Ojogbo Ẹlimi: Ẹ̀sán word for 'Dreadful Spirit.' '*Ojogbo*' means 'something dreadful', while '*Ẹlimi*' means 'spirit'.

35. Ikhimi: Ẹ̀sán word for Egyptian Balsam, a tree native to much of Africa. In most parts of southern Nigeria, it is often referred to as

the king of trees and is believed by some to have magical powers.

36. Ọgbọnọ: Nigerian soup made from ground dried African (wild) mango seeds. Popular in mostly southern Nigeria.

37. Pounded yam: Nigerian food native to many ethnic groups in southern Nigeria. It is prepared by pounding boiled yam with mortar and pestle.

38. Here Nẹnẹ's song translates into:

My mother's food

This is not my mother's food

39. Amẹbọ: Nigerian expression used to describe a loose tongued person. A gossip.

40. Osukhamẹdin: Ẹsán word used to refer to the stock from a harvested palm fruit head.

41. Ọnaiwu: Edo name, meaning, "This

will not die."

42. Wrapper: A piece of fabric wrapped around the waist.

Printed in Great Britain
by Amazon